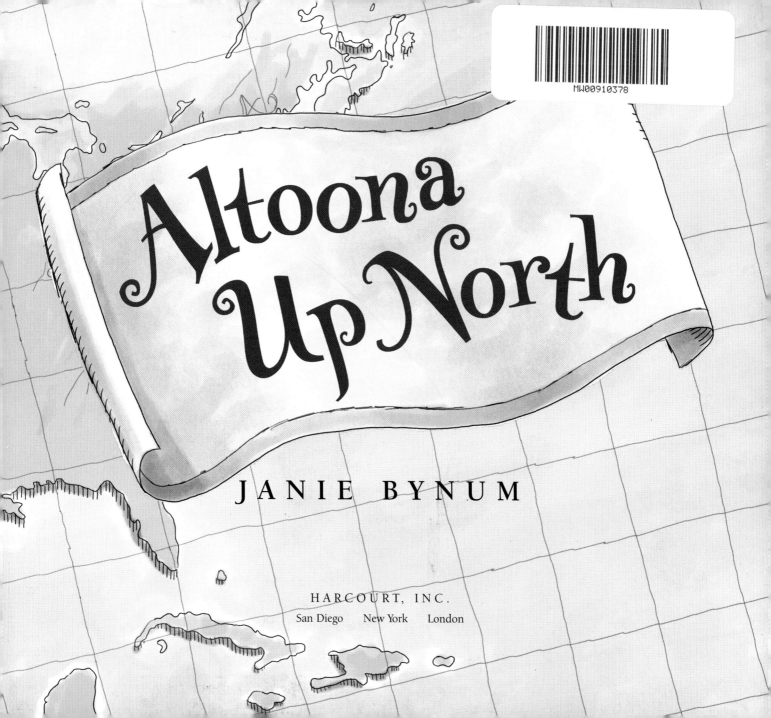

Altoona Up North

JANIE BYNUM

HARCOURT, INC.

San Diego   New York   London

Requests for permission to make copies of any part of the work should be
mailed to the following address: Permissions Department, Harcourt, Inc.,
6277 Sea Harbor Drive, Orlando, Florida 32887-6777.

www.harcourt.com

Library of Congress Cataloging-in-Publication Data
Bynum, Janie.
Altoona up north/Janie Bynum.
p. cm.
Summary: Altoona the baboon goes to visit her aunt in the frigid north,
but after some adventures in the snow, Auntie gives everyone a warm surprise.
[1. Aunts—Fiction. 2. Baboons—Fiction. 3. Cold—Fiction. 4. Stories in rhyme.]
I. Title
PZ8.3.B9935An 2001
[E]—dc21 00-10899
ISBN 0-15-202313-5

C E G I K J H F D B

Manufactured in China

The illustrations in this book were done in digital pen-and-ink and watercolor.
The display type was hand lettered by Janie Bynum.
The text type was set in Berkeley Old Style.
Color separations by Bright Arts Ltd., Hong Kong
Manufactured by South China Printing Company, Ltd., China
This book was printed on totally chlorine-free Nymolla Matte Art paper.
Production supervision by Sandra Grebenar and Ginger Boyer
Designed by Linda Lockowitz

To Paul—
thanks for the journey

To my parents—
thanks for the gear

Altoona Baboona
gets mail on her dune-a.
Her dear aunt is lonely
in north Saskatoon-a.

So Altoona and friends
prepare for a ride.
They buy some warm clothes
and a good travel guide.

The travelers fly north,
watching green turn to white,
through rainfall and snowstorm,
through daytime and night.

They land on a hilltop
and trek across snow,
to where Auntie is waiting
with scones and cocoa.

They hug and they visit.

They ice-fish for pike.

They enter a sled race

and go for a hike.

Auntie tries to keep up,
but she's tired of the cold.
Her hipbones are aching.
She's feeling too old. . . .

"I've got an idea,"
  Auntie says to the three.
"Just half a day south,
  there's a nice place to ski."

Altoona takes lessons,
Raccoon-a skis hills,

while Auntie and Loon-a
find easier thrills.

"Now, let's rent a boat."
Auntie's scheme is airtight.
"There's a cabin downriver,
    where we'll spend the night."

The cabin is musty
and smells like a sock.
The bed is too lumpy
and hard as a rock!

The next day they're grumpy.
They've not slept a wink—
because of that bed
and the damp and the stink!

A farmer drives by,
tips his hat, says, "Goo'day,"
then sells them his horse
and his cart full of hay.

The horse plods along.
The friends take a nap,
while Auntie gets busy
with compass and map.

When the cart finally stops,
the sun has gone down.
Auntie wakes up the friends
and leads them to town.

Sly Auntie sneaks out
as the sun starts to rise.
Her plan has gone well,
so she springs her surprise. . . .

When the travelers awake
and step out the door,
they suddenly realize
they've been here before!

And there on the dock
Auntie waits with a smile.
"Surprise! We're back home.
Let's *fly* the last mile!"

They enjoyed their adventures.
Snow skiing was fun.
But it's good to be home,
back to sand, surf, and sun.

So Altoona Baboona,
she still shares her dune-a,
her heart and her home,
with Raccoon-a and Loon-a . . .

. . . and now with her auntie
from north Saskatoon-a!

Saskatoon

Swift Current

Crowsnest Pass

Flat Head

Lost Trail
Resort

Cold Comfort
Cabins

Coyote Lake

Laguna Beach